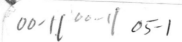
00-1 '00-1 05-1

ORANGE CITY PUBLIC LIBRARY
Orange City, IA

1. Items are returnable on the date printed on the due date slip in this pocket. Items may be renewed once except books on reserve.

2. Magazines may be kept one week and may be renewed once for the same period.

3. A fine of five cents a day will be charged on each item which is not returned on its due date.

4. All injuries to any library materials beyond reasonable wear, and all losses shall be made good to the satisfaction of the Librarian.

DEMCO

Hero for Hire

DONNA TAUSCHER

SCHOLASTIC INC.
New York Toronto London Auckland Sydney

Cover art by Maren

ISBN 0-590-18901-8

12 11 10 9 8 7 6 5 4 3 2 1   8 9/9 0 1 2 3/0

Printed in the U.S.A.
First Scholastic printing, July 1998

Hero for Hire

PROLOGUE

Han Solo is in trouble. Recently freed from carbonite by Princess Leia, he is locked in a small, dark cell in the dungeon of Jabba the Hutt's palace. He is awaiting a death sentence. If that's not enough, he's suffering from hibernation sickness — nausea, blindness, and confused thoughts. Not to mention he doesn't know what has happened to Princess Leia. Obviously, he is in no condition to escape. And not even Chewbacca's presence in the cell with him offers much hope.

In the meantime, Han's presence has come to the attention of a monk, Sai'da, of the B'omarr order of monks. The B'omarr monks live in the very core of the mysterious palace where Jabba the Hutt has unlawfully staked his claim in the outer rooms. The B'omarr monks built this palace as a monastery, but eventually withdrew into the inner sanctum. They have an uneasy peace with Jabba.

Sai'da is a historian. He has a quest for knowledge of species outside of his limited sphere. He hears stories of the Rebel Alliance and of the Empire. Yet he rarely has the opportunity to talk with those involved in the daily struggles. He wonders what motivates someone to join forces with one side or the other. How does an individual life unfold and take shape? How does this affect history?

These are some of the questions that Sai'da ponders as he approaches the cell of Han Solo, led by one of Jabba's guards. Sai'da is a tall, thin man draped in a dark robe that covers his head. He walks quietly, arms crossed, with his head tilted to the side, contemplating the coming interview. He attempts no conversation with the guard. He has a data pad in one hand that he will activate as soon as he enters the cell. All conversations will be recorded for future consideration.

Sai'da, like most highly trained B'omarr monks, has unique, mystical insight into the nature of others. He senses this will be a most interesting exchange.

Sai'da: Greetings, Mr. Solo, I am Sai'da, a historian of the B'omarr order of monks. We built this monastery —

Han: Whoa. I don't think I'll be needing any religious assistance in my final hours, buddy, since I don't plan on staying here long enough to become an appetizer for Jabba's rancor.

Sai'da: No, you misunderstand. It's your history I want. I'm not here to minister to you in your final hours.

Han: Chewie, would you mind showing our new friend to the door? I've got some problems, mister, and telling you how I got here won't help them any. No offense. Besides, I'm having a hard time even keeping my head up at the moment. I'm pretty woozy, and, oh yeah, in case you missed it, I'm blind. Chewie, help me sit down before you toss this guy out of here.

Sai'da: There's no need for violence. I am not

your jailer. Besides, I'm locked up in here with you now. I don't have access to the cell. One of Jabba's guards let me in.

Han: That still doesn't sound too friendly to me. You and the guard are pals, right? Never mind, I don't want to hear it.

Sai'da: The guard and I are not acquainted. I only wish to speak with you. Since my order cultivates patience, I have time to wait. You don't, however, seem to be feeling too well. Is it the hibernation sickness?

Han: So, you know a few things, huh? If you've got some answers, you can have a seat. Like how long is this gonna last? Or even better, tell me what happened to Princess Leia.

Chewbacca: Grrrrrlwaugh!!

Han: It's okay, pal. I'm sorry I didn't tell you about our princess. But finding you in the cell was a shock. Plus I was pretty disoriented. Not to mention nauseated. But really, she's okay. She was very much alive when she got me out of the carbonite.

We were barely reunited, though, when Jabba's ugly laugh surprised us. A short-lived rescue. And since he's not one to listen to reason — big surprise — next thing you know his goons have hauled me to this wet, leaky, poor excuse of a cell, and I don't know where she is. So, what's your name again, monk man?

Sai'da: Sai'da.

Han: Okay, Sai'da. Tell me where the princess is.

Sai'da: As far as I know, she is with Jabba. She is unharmed. It is for you he harbors his animosity.

Han: Animosity? That's a polite way of putting it. I like how you educated types talk. I mean, I'm here waiting for Jabba's spineless thugs to show up and you say . . . never mind. Listen, the point is, you don't think the princess is in danger?

Sai'da: I can't be sure of anything with Jabba, but I don't believe she is in danger for now.

Han: For now. Not good enough. Can you get us to her? I know I don't look like I'm in any shape for a big rescue attempt, but my best buddy here, Chewie, can handle the physical stuff.

Chewbacca: Grrrrwwwl!

Sai'da: I don't want to mislead you. I am in no position to take you to the princess. I am here simply to record your history and —

Han: Maybe I'd feel a little more like talking if I thought there was something in it for me. You know your way around this place, right? But, hey, how come you're in this monastery — you did say it was a monastery, right?

Sai'da: Correct.

Han: Got to be the weirdest monastery in

the galaxy. Anyway, if you're not with Jabba, what's your deal? Why should I be wasting my time with you?

Sai'da: Time cannot be wasted, Mr. Solo. Let me explain my presence. The B'omarr order of monks built this monastery as a place of perfect exile. It is vast. We eventually withdrew into the inner sanctum as our practices do not require much space. We focus on the power of the mind and spirit. Unfortunately, people began to break into the citadel and to use its corridors and alcoves for business purposes and hideaways. Jabba the Hutt eventually claimed a portion of our monastery as his "palace." We rarely see him. We study our philosophies and keep our private peace.

Han: Peace, huh? You've got your peace while Jabba's wreaking havoc on half the galaxy?

Sai'da: He is not our concern.

Han: Well, he's my concern, monk man, and if you're not pals with Jabba, how come you know I'm here?

Sai'da: We monks are aware of all that goes on in the palace. We have a mystical intuition into the inner lives of certain people. You have come to my attention. I am a historian and I am interested in your history.

Jabba accommodates some of our requests

as he has a primitive fear of our powers. He provided me with access to your cell.

Han: Jabba's afraid of something? That's a good one. You might just be somebody I want to know after all. So, tell me, were you aware of me and my history while I was doing my act as the frozen man?

Sai'da: Yes, but only vaguely.

Han: And this intuition you have? Can you use it to tell me about Leia?

Sai'da: I can tell you that she has a powerful force inside her that is not diminished by captivity.

Han: I could have pretty much told you that myself. I was thinking of something a little more helpful. But still . . . what do you think, Chewie?

Chewbacca: Waurrgh. Rrmph.

Han: Maybe. The monk knows this place better than we do, that's for sure. I guess we don't have anything to lose. You seem to be our only option, Sai'da, my man.

Sai'da: As I said, I don't wish to raise your hopes. I am a historian and I seek to record your story. My usefulness as an escape artist is, I'm afraid, limited. To put it mildly.

Han: At least you're honest. Maybe. But do you think you could answer a few questions along the way?

Sai'da: Perhaps. As I'm able.

Han: All right, you can start by telling me what you look like.

Sai'da: That's irrelevant. Only the mind matters.

Han: Are you kidding me? You've been in this dungeon too long, mister, trust me. Try getting yourself frozen up in carbonite for . . . how long was I a wall ornament, Chewie?

Chewbacca: Awwrk.

Han: A year? A year. I'm surprised my brain hasn't turned into a big piece of slug gel.

Whew. I'm not enjoying this. Being blind. I feel cornered, like someone could come at me and I'd never know what hit me. It's not how I'm used to operating. How long exactly do you think I'll be this way?

Sai'da: I'm afraid that, once again, I can be of no help. I heard that you were suffering from hibernation sickness, but I have no idea how long it lasts. I believe your time in carbonite was a bit of an experiment.

Han: Great. That's helpful.

Sai'da: I apologize for my lack of knowledge in this area. Perhaps as you're waiting for your sight to return, you could begin telling me a bit of your history.

Han: Didn't you just say something a while ago about you monks studying your private philosophies and keeping to yourselves?

Sai'da: As a historian, I am a bit different from my fellow monks. By necessity I have an interest in that which takes place beyond my order. It is sometimes a struggle, this difference in outlook.

Han: I can relate to that. I'm an outsider myself. In any case, I guess I'm stuck sitting here. It's not like I'm going to plan a big escape in this condition. Maybe I oughta just talk to you and get my mind off the situation. Maybe you'll see what a swell kind of guy I am and be a little more helpful.

No comment? That's okay. You've got the patience and I've got the time.

Well, now, I've never been a reflective kind of guy, but now that I think about it, you've caught me — so to speak — at a good time. I haven't had much of a chance to chat lately, master mind, so I suppose it wouldn't hurt to make some sense out of all this. At least if I die, the Han Solo legend will live on.

Chewbacca: Varawrk!

Han: Not funny, Chewie. Hey, I haven't officially introduced you to Chewbacca, my first mate. I'm sure he'll have a few things to say unless he's changed a lot this past year. Seems like other people have changed, right, Chewie? Ha!

If what Chewbacca says is true, Luke Skywalker is now a Jedi Knight and he's going to rescue us at any moment. That makes me laugh. I find it highly unlikely that the kid can pull that off even if he is calling himself a Jedi these days. He did say this himself, huh, Chewie?

Chewbacca: Vrowwf.

Han: A lot of changes happen in a year. I might even believe him if he gets us out of this creepy palace. Let's hope he at least finds Leia. The thought of that slimy, overstuffed gangster toad touching her . . .

Chewbacca: Gggrrowwwl!!

Han: It's okay, buddy. She'll be fine. You said Luke's on the way. Who knows? The kid has had some amazing moments, I have to admit.

DATA PAD ENTRY 2

Han: Okay, where do I start? If what you want is a historical record, I suspect it has more to do with the Rebel Alliance than with just this scoundrel's adventures, as fascinating as they might be. So I'll start with right before I met old Ben and the kid.

I'm a smuggler. Might as well set you straight on that right away. Don't want you thinking I'm some kind of dedicated Alliance hero. I'll own up to my past.

Sai'da: The smuggling is behind you now?

Han: I don't know. It's starting to look that way.

Anyway, back before I met up with my current Rebel pals I was too busy trying to keep the *Millennium Falcon* and Chewie and me afloat, moneywise, to give a lot of thought to the Rebel Alliance. The *Falcon* takes some major upkeep because she's the fastest ship in the galaxy, and that isn't braggin'. Ever since I won her in a — shall we say — game of chance, I've tried to do good by her. You don't come by a ship like her very often.

I wasn't giving a lot of thought to the Rebels in my smuggling days. Not that I was a supporter of the Imperial Forces either. Absolutely not. They were always trying to shut me down. I just tried to steer clear of any situation involving the Imperials or the Rebels. Politics didn't interest me. Survival did.

My one encounter with the Rebel Alliance was not a happy one. This is kind of off the subject, but you should know that there were reasons I wasn't feeling real thrilled with the Rebel forces. You see, I risked my neck to help this old friend . . . okay, this pretty, young woman. Her name was Bria Tharen. Anyway, she convinced me to help her and her Alliance buddies, and I convinced my friends to help, too. Now, maybe you can't call a bunch of smugglers friends, exactly, but the smuggler's code means something. It's a kind of friendship.

I hadn't seen Bria for a long time. And then she shows up in my life as an agent for the Rebellion. I wasn't listening to any of her "Let's help the cause, Han" nonsense. Until she started talking money. More money than I'd ever dreamed of having. She knew how to get to me.

Bria had a good plan. The Hutt lords on Yle-sia had stockpiled a huge supply of the best glitterstim. The Rebellion needed money and needed it bad. The plan was simple: steal the spice and sell it to the Hutt crimelords. If my buddies and I would help, we would get half the high-class spice as reward. Now that would light a spark to any smuggler's ambition. And it did. It took me no time to round up a crew.

So far, so good, right? Not for long. I won't bore you with the details of just how tricky this deal turned out to be. Let's just say it was more than a simple theft, and it involved a lot of fighting. And when we finally get to the spice warehouses, what do you think happens? Bria and her fellow idealists take all the best glitter-stim and leave the second-class spice for us, the low-life smugglers.

If I thought I had some tenuous friendships, well, I could kiss them good-bye. My pals turned on me in a flash. Refused to believe I didn't know how this would turn out ahead of time. My so-called betrayal made them truly furious. They thought I was in on the deal with Bria. You want to talk about some seri-ously bad attitudes. They blamed me for her treachery!

And she was treacherous. Bria was so com-pletely into the Rebel Alliance that she just had to use me one more time before taking off. Am

I a sucker, or what? So when she said she knew where the High Priests stored their treasures and asked if I could help. . . . Yep, even after that spice fiasco I thought I was gonna pocket a few jewels. Think again. The minute we found that treasure and I reached for a share, she pulled a blaster on me! Said she was sorry, but the Alliance needed it more than I did, what with having to buy ships and weapons. Gratitude was not her strong suit, that one.

Sai'da: But she deeply believed in the Alliance? Isn't this a human trait, allegiance?

Han: Yes! But that's not the point! Sure, she went on and on about the Empire planning something big and the Rebels having to stop them. She was sincere. But she lied to me! You've got to be able to trust people and she didn't show me that the Rebels were people you could trust. I lost my friends, and I didn't make any credits on top of it.

Chewbacca: Ahhhhroarr.

Han: You're right, Chewie, I didn't lose all my friends. I still had my best buddy, my first mate. But I was not in a good mood, to say the least.

Anyway, you understand now why my history with the Rebels was not a particularly trusting one. I'm not talking politics here. Just plain old human interaction.

I'm the kind of guy who likes to keep to himself and avoid entanglements. Not that that's always possible. There's always someone you gotta deal with or take a chance on. I don't have to like it, though.

All right, history man, I'm tired and I've just started. I don't know if it's the carbonite or just telling you about my first minor foray with the Rebels. I'm not exactly used to talking. Living inside your head is not an easy deal, even if you seem to think it is.

Anyway, I heard later that Bria was killed in a raid. That shook me up. I mean, even after her betrayal I still cared about her.

And now. Well, here I sit with Leia captured and awaiting who knows what fate. Do you think she's in some miserable cell like this one? Is Jabba leaving her alone?

Sai'da: Mr. Solo, I recommend focusing on the fact that your princess is alive. This is all I know.

Han: I wish I could pull myself together. And stop thinking about the here and now. But it isn't easy. I keep thinking about the princess. So I won't stop asking you for help as long as she's a prisoner. Got it?

Han: So, forget my problem with the Rebels for the time being. Back to the first point of this story, which is meeting the old man and the kid — the trouble duo. I would have avoided them if I hadn't been desperate for money. Story of my life.

Your neighbor, Jabba the Hutt, was not happy with me after I dumped a load of spice I was smuggling for him. He's not a very understanding kind of guy. He didn't much care that the Imperials had boarded me and I didn't want to spend the rest of my life being tortured by a bunch of goons. I'm funny like that.

I really thought I'd find that load of spice I'd jettisoned. Dream on.

So Jabba's on my tail, pestering me to pay up for the loss, and I'm slinking around Mos Eisley avoiding him and trying to wrangle up some cash. To tell the truth, I wasn't looking at much work when Chewbacca here tells me there's money to be had off these two characters in Chaimun's cantina. Chewie's hooting about some fresh-faced kid right off the farm and an old coot with a lightsaber. A lightsaber, believe it or not. I was thinking, "Who uses one of those antiques anymore?" But Chewie said the old man knew how to use it. It was no gimmick. Pulled it on a couple of brawlers who were threatening the kid and took 'em apart.

What did I care? Promise of a little money and I was heading to the cantina to check it out.

It's pretty hard to look out of place in that outlaw haven, but they managed. I had this feeling in my gut when I met those two, like this whole simple trip to Alderaan was going to be more than I bargained for.

But with Jabba ready to sic the bounty hunters on me, I didn't have much choice. The 17,000 credit fee — I couldn't believe it: I only asked for 10,000, but the old man says he'll give me 2,000 and then 15,000 more on Alderaan. Not bad for a clip across space.

And what's the cargo? Two humans and two droids. And no Imperial entanglements. Simple, huh? Shoulda known right then that they had some kind of a bounty on them. Worse, it turns out.

You'd have thought when the Imperial goons

showed up looking for them in the cantina I would have been a little more alert. I could have told them right then, "Hey, boys, this is more trouble than I need right now." But I had the 17,000 dangling in front of me like some hypnotic mind tease, so I let my guard down.

It's weird how you know stuff about people and you can't even admit it to yourself at the time. Sure it was the money, but I gotta admit that as much as the kid irritated me, he also got under my skin in a funny way. I wanted to teach him a thing or two. He was too naive. He had a smart mouth. He was still wet behind the ears, but talking about how 17,000 was too much for the trip. How he could buy his own ship for that. When I asked who was going to fly the thing, he got all indignant, like he was some super ace pilot.

I see kids like him all the time. A lot of hot air and chest thumping and nothing to back it up. They don't last long. I just wanted to see if this kid was any different.

Talk about different — the old man, he was like some walking legend or something with his cape and lightsaber. He had a strange look in his eye. But he was all business, a straight shooter in that department. It was an easy transaction. Still, there was something weird . . . an intensity that you don't see much around Mos Eisley.

Most people around the spaceport act like they don't care about anything, and most of them don't. Unless they take a dislike to you. Then you know it.

These two stood out. They interested me. And not necessarily in a good way.

And my ship interested them. It should've. The *Millennium Falcon*. I told you a little about her. She's a beauty. Okay, a little rough on the eyes, but nobody's got her spirit. She's a modified Corellian stock light freighter. Boy, is she modified. Chewie and I put nothing but work into her. And even though the Jedi duo had never heard of her, most people in Mos Eisley had. She had a reputation all over the galaxy. It's the ship that made the Kessel run in less than twelve parsecs!

She's a ship to get excited over, Sai'da; one in a million.

Han: If I had any doubts about taking off for the Alderaan system in the *Falcon* with my strange new cargo, it was quickly dispelled. Greedo showed up at my table at the cantina as soon as Ben and Luke left.

Are you following this, historian? Ben and Luke are the old man and the kid. Wanna keep you straight. And Greedo is this mindless, Rodian lug who works for Jabba. Killer for hire. Got it? Okay.

Greedo is all puffed up like one of those poisonous Eberon spiders about to capture his prey. He says that Jabba has a hefty bounty on me all because of this spice deal. I try to explain that I'm good for the money. Greedo is picturing his pockets lined with Jabba's reward, though, and I can see right away my minutes are numbered.

It's not that I like eliminating unsavory characters in my free time, you know, but I'm not gonna let myself be had either. I chatted with him in a real friendly way. He wasn't as smart as he was greedy. I pulled a blaster out from under the table real easy and Greedo was no more.

That's the trouble with Jabba's flunkies and with most of the cretins who work for the crime-lords. They can't use their heads. Or whatever part of their anatomy their pea brains are located in. Gives me one up on 'em.

I figured that wasn't the end of Jabba's little harassment scheme. Chewie and I hightailed it back to Docking Bay 94, the *Falcon*'s humble home. We were prepared for some follow-up action, but not for the arrival of the king of ooze himself, Jabba. That's how important I was to Jabba's self-esteem. Trust me. It was about more than money. He didn't want anybody thinking I'd pulled one over on him by not paying for the spice foul-up.

Jabba was in the docking bay with every imaginable kind of alien scum in tow. He was calling my name. I answered from behind and startled the whole motley bunch. I figured if Jabba was with them he wasn't looking for murder right then. His henchmen tend to that dirty work these days.

I showed Jabba some real attitude. It's the only thing that gets his attention. You want to show no fear in front of that slavering hulk. You've seen him, right? You never get used to how disgusting a creature he is. Shocks me every time. Not that he would know it. Sometimes survival is 50 percent show, putting up a good front.

He's acting like he's distressed about Greedo's demise. That he thought the two of us were friends. He's got some pretty good attitude, too. We both knew he was talking fantasy land. I told him I would pay him back, but I needed time. He agreed for an additional 20 percent. Of course, he said if I didn't come through this time there would be a price on my head so large that I wouldn't be able to go near a civilized system for the rest of my life. Now *that* I believed. I assured him it would be my pleasure to pay him back.

In my mind I was picturing the bounty hunter, Boba Fett, tracking me down. You don't even want to know about Boba. You've led a sheltered life, Sai'da, even in this sicko palace, if you haven't met Boba Fett. Just hearing about Boba would fracture your peace of mind. I don't even want to think about him.

So, as you can imagine, Chewie and I were a bit anxious to take on our weird little crew and make it to Alderaan pronto.

Han: The *Falcon* was almost ready and I was dreaming of retiring for a while to someplace Jabba the Hutt hadn't heard about. I know a few planets in the outer system that are so small and out of the way that you could almost have one to yourself. I was thinking a little down-time on one of these would suit me just fine. Right. Fat chance.

So, I was tinkering on the *Falcon* and in-dulging my little fantasy, when the old man and the kid arrived with the droids in tow. With *much more* than them in tow, actually.

It's a good thing I can shift gears in a hurry.

Chewbacca: Mphwramph.

Han: What's going on, buddy? You still think you should have seen it coming? Should have checked it out when you let our little band of fugitives in? Stop blaming yourself for missing the spy who was tailing them.

Sai'da, you might as well know now how sensitive this big old Wookiee can be.

One thing's for sure, though, somebody didn't have a problem making some coin from the Empire. The Imperials knew exactly when the Rebel party arrived. The kid barely had time to insult the *Falcon*. "A piece of junk," I think he called it. I hate ignorance. I mean, she'll make point five past lightspeed!

But there's no point getting riled up in retrospect.

Everybody got on board pronto and Chewbacca was readying the engines while I made a final inspection on the outside. Suddenly, the door flew open and Imperial stormtroopers entered with blasters firing. I managed to down a few of the royal scum so I could make my way into the *Falcon*. Thanks to Chewie here my new traveling pals and I were in the airspace over Mos Eisley in record time.

Have you ever seen Imperial stormtroopers?

Sai'da: I have heard of them only. Are they of interest?

Han: Oh, yeah. Weird guys, covered in shiny white armor with helmets. You never see their faces. They all look exactly alike. Act exactly alike. I guess that's the point. The Empire doesn't even want them to look human. I mean, they're ready at any moment to give their lives for the Empire. They're like upright insects coming at you, swarms of them. Droids look more real to me than stormtroopers.

Anyway, once we were in space, things really got interesting. It wasn't enough that the Imperial stormtroopers followed my cargo to the docking bay, but they came after us in Imperial cruisers. Okay, I'm not slow. I was getting the idea about just how hot our passengers were. You'd think they might have mentioned that the Imperial forces were after them.

Three cruisers were coming up fast on us. The old man stayed calm. But the kid — no surprise — was being a giant pain. He's yelling, "Why don't you outrun them? I thought you said this thing was fast." Like jumping into hyperspace doesn't take a few calculations! As I told the kid, "It ain't like dusting crops, boy."

We outmaneuvered those cruisers and then, bam, made the jump. In a flash I had us free and clear. The kid would have still been down on the Mos Eisley space station looking to buy a ship and talking about how tough he was if I hadn't been around.

You know, I kind of like talking about this. I was afraid my brain was never going to defrost and my past would just be some hazy story that happened to someone else. Not that I wouldn't mind forgetting *some* of my past. I think I had too much time in carbonite. Because things are looking different to me now than they used to.

Sai'da: How so? I'm curious about the carbonite experience. I'm wondering what kind of altered state it might have produced in you, and if it's something like one of the B'omarr meditations. Do you want to discuss your time in carbonite now?

Han: Not right now. Later, maybe, if you don't get too mystical on me. Right now I'd just like to rest a minute.

Listen, Sai'da, do you think you could at least get a message to Leia? She might feel a little better knowing I'm alive and with Chewbacca.

Sai'da: I suppose I could devise a way to get a message to her. Perhaps when I leave the cell, somehow, I could . . . I'm not sure. I detect that you and the princess are more than comrades. Correct?

Han: I guess so. I hope so. It's been a year since I've really seen her. But when I came out of hibernation and realized someone had freed me but I didn't know who, I asked, "Who are you?" And she said, "Someone who loves you."

Chewbacca: Rrrphmmmaff.

Han: Yeah, yeah, Chewie. Take it easy.

But it was good to hear those words. We've had a pretty rocky time of it, me and Leia. She's as difficult as I am, if you can believe it. And now I wonder if I'll ever see her again.

Sai'da: One can never tell what will happen in the future. For now, Mr. Solo, I will try to send the princess a short message. A hello from two prisoners. Nothing more.

Han: Thank you.

Han: Well, I was pretty happy there for a while, having escaped Mos Eisley and the Imperial ships. I was advancing on Alderaan and the answer to my cash flow problem, and the *Falcon* was unscathed after another close call.

You know, I didn't pay much attention to the droids on the trip. That was before I understood the dynamite that Artoo-Detoo was storing in his loyal little droid innards. Those were the good old days before I'd ever heard the name, the Death Star. And to think I called the kid naive. Right. Well, looking back I was pretty naive myself.

The droids were a trip in themselves. Artoo was easy to take. Kind of a funny little guy somehow. He pretty much kept to himself. But his buddy, Threepio, he was something else. He's an arrogant one, considering he's a walking metallic device! Oh, he's got his circuits stuffed with information, all right.

You'd like him 'cause he'd be happy to talk to you for as long as you could stand it. Speaks all kinds of languages. He can even tell you the customs of species from all over the galaxy. Unfortunately, he won't shut up sometimes. He babbles on and on until you wish you knew where the deactivation button was for his vocabulator. Seriously. He can really get on your nerves.

Speaking of getting on your nerves. . . .

There we were, heading for Alderaan, safe and sound, and suddenly, I was feeling a little underappreciated. Don't laugh. I guess I feel that way a lot. No one had said, "Hey, Han, thanks for being as good as your word," or anything. Sure I was getting paid, but that's not the point. I'd just pulled off a pretty slick escape and they were acting like it was chump change.

I don't know. Maybe the point is just that I'm making excuses for how irritating I found the old man and the kid. There we are, cooped up together, and you'd think they might have something interesting to say.

No. The old man was too busy training the kid, Luke, in how to get in touch with the Force. You see, Ben had given the kid a lightsaber, just like the one he'd whacked those creeps with in the cantina. An old-fashioned tube of light is all it is. Ben was teaching him how to ward off blasts from the seeker droid floating in front of him. He could have just given him a blaster and told him to eliminate it! It would have been a lot easier.

But no, he's saying stuff like, "a Jedi can feel the Force flowing through him." And Luke is dead earnest trying to feel this Force. It was more than *this* man could take. I told them I'd been around the galaxy more than either of them and even though I'd seen a lot of strange stuff, I'd never seen any one all-powerful Force controlling everything. I said it was all hokey religion, that there was no mystical energy controlling my destiny.

They just ignored me.

But to tell you the truth, what I said wasn't exactly what I believe. Let me gather my thoughts a minute, okay? All this talking is pretty exhausting. That hibernation was no vacation.

Maybe this is it: I know about knowing what you don't know. Oh, great, that's as clear as a meteor shower. Let me try again. I've got this reputation for being lucky, you know? Blasters have missed me by milliseconds. I've left the wrong place at exactly the right time more than once in my life. It's like if my life is threatened, I know in the moment how to save myself. I guess you could call it intuition. I can get out of scrapes by the narrowest of margins.

Chewbacca: Rowwrrk!

Han: Ahhh, Chewie, this little scrape ain't over yet either. Besides, sometimes you know a situation is going to be bad, real bad, and you can't stay out of it because other people are involved. Life's gettin' real complicated, ain't it, buddy?

So, anyway, I told Ben how there wasn't a mystical Force at work in the universe. I was so sure that when things turned out right, it was simple luck. But now, looking back, I think he was probably right. He said there was no such thing as luck. That old guy knew his stuff, it turned out. I wish I'd have talked to him a little more instead of being so, well, so me. Ha!

I'll bet he could have told some tales about the Clone Wars. I'd heard stories about the Jedi Knights, but I thought they were long gone. So at the time I wasn't sure the old man wasn't just some delusional desert hermit. And if that was the case, I didn't want him encouraging Luke. The kid had enough trouble with that attitude and smart mouth of his.

Chewbacca: Rhhrrmuph.

Han: Yeah, Chewie, at least we had something in common. Makes me laugh to think about it.

But the old man, Ben Kenobi, I guess my intuition was right about him, too. Because something told me that he was the real deal. I just didn't *want* to believe all that gibberish.

Yet, I listened to him. I think because he trusted me right away. Trust is not something I shared with people in my line of work. Most of the people I work for trust one thing — money. Everybody's on the lookout for who's cheating who. But old Ben, Obi-Wan Kenobi, he accepted that I was as good as my word. It made me uneasy. He seemed to think I was more than a smuggler and vagabond. And that's not just conjecture on my part.

Sai'da: What did he think you were?

Han: Good question. I don't know exactly. Except that he told Luke when he met me that I wasn't just another Corellian smuggler or some minor outlaw. Oh, sure, maybe that doesn't sound exactly like praise to you, but I thought it was pretty perceptive. I'd worked hard to put up that front and the old man saw right through it. I'm telling you, he could turn those strange eyes of his on you and *know* you. At least it seemed that way. Kind of gave me the spooks, the way he looked at me — like he saw an alternative fate for me.

I guess I saw myself as different from most people I associated with, too. Not that I put a lot of time and effort into thinking about it. I didn't exactly sit around meditating like you religious types, wondering about the state of my soul. It was more like wondering about my next meal.

Ahhh, I don't know.

At the time I wasn't admitting to all this. Not me. It's amazing how my mouth just keeps flinging insults and challenges even when I haven't exactly figured the situation out yet.

Mainly it's because I don't want people to know what I'm thinking. You gotta be careful. People go sincere on you and if you fall for it they can sucker you into anything. You always gotta wonder what's really up with people and keep them guessing about you. That's a simple survival technique when you're a smuggler. A habit.

Besides, even if you're fighting to save the galaxy, you need a sense of humor. Remind me to remind Luke about a sense of humor, Chewie. That kid is too serious for his own good sometimes.

Chewbacca: Rowwwgh.

Han: Right. We know how to keep it light if we need to, Chewie, my man.

Hey, what's that? Oh, don't tell me — Jabba and his freak show. What a racket. I'm just gonna put that out of my head. I don't even want to imagine what's goin' on. Not like I could do anything about it. Or could I? What do you think, Sai'da, my friend?

33

Sai'da: I don't think you want to know.

Han: Know what? Hey — if Leia's in trouble I'm not going to sit in here droning on. I need out. And your little history project will *be* history, if you catch my drift.

Sai'da: Please calm down, Mr. Solo. I wasn't referring to Princess Leia. It's just that there is terror invoked by Jabba that is best left unspoken. Especially in situations like this when nothing can be done.

Han: If I could get out of here then something could be done! I'm getting fed up. What good does it do me or Leia talking to you?

Sai'da: I understand. Perhaps when I get the message to Leia, I can also bring word of her well-being to you. I am not without sympathy for your desire to help the princess and to free yourself.

Han: That would be good. A start, at least. Whew. This is a tough one, just sitting here talking and not being able to even see. And those noises! I mean, I know you're a monk, but I don't see how you can stand it. Tell me, do you ever get any rest in this place? It doesn't sound much like a monastery.

Sai'da: We are able to retreat into ourselves. When we do so, we are unaware of the sounds produced by the outside world.

I know it is difficult, but perhaps if we returned to the story of Luke and Ben during the

Falcon's passage from Mos Eisley to Alderaan, you would forget for a while.

Han: I'll never forget what's going on in this place, believe me. But I'll keep talking. It's better than thinking about Jabba's tricks.

Okay. Where was I? The old man, right? You know, at least one thing Ben had to say interested me — something unusual. He knew his stuff about Wookiees. A lot of people think Wookiees are just giant furballs. They don't get it. But Ben treated Chewie decently right away. He even taught me a few things I wasn't aware of, like how ancient the Wookiee culture is.

Chewie had talked to me some about his close ties to nature. I just didn't realize how ingrained it was in Wookiee culture. Ben called it a "sympathetic vibration" with the natural world.

Sai'da: Interesting. There is much ancient history that refers to this type of close relationship to nature. It is assumed that as cities and space stations claimed the inhabitants of nature's realm, this gift was lost. Perhaps not fully, however.

Han: Well, I guess that's what Ben was on to, learned one. I'm pretty sure you and the old man would have had a lot to talk about.

Anyway, Chewie was playing a holo-game with Artoo, the little droid with secrets, but he was listening to the old man say a few words about Wookieedom. I think this might explain Chewie's initial enthusiasm for the Rebels.

Chewbacca: Narrowwl.

Han: I thought so, buddy. Ben also said that Wookiees have an affinity for the Force. I think it has something to do with the nature thing. Anyway, he found Chewie a lot more complicated and interesting than most people. You can tell a lot about a person from how they treat a Wookiee.

I was almost starting to like the old guy when we got into a little argument about money. Not that he wasn't going to pay me, just that he found my pursuit of money "trifling." Give me a break. Maybe he didn't need anything living like a desert monk — no offense — but making your way around the galaxy requires something a little more worldly, like money.

He seemed amused by my need for it. And so did Luke. Because anything the old man said, Luke thought was written on some holy tablet or something. My nerves were getting all worked up. I got over that soon enough, though, when the bad news hit.

And let me tell you, the bad news happened fast once we came out of hyperspace.

Han: We cleared hyperspace at exactly the right point to arrive at Alderaan. I started to relax, thinking this was one weird trip that was over. I was expecting a clear view and an easy ride from here on out.

No way. There was an intense storm of what looked like meteors racing toward us, battering the *Falcon*. We were completely confused. And the big question was: Where was Alderaan?

I'll tell you where she was: Gone. Finito. The craziest thing I've ever seen. Someone had somehow blasted her into nothing but a billion pieces of flying rock. Seriously, where there should have been an entire, peaceful planet there was nothing. There wasn't much time to even think about the magnitude of it, though, because this Imperial fighter came ripping by us out of nowhere. And before we could figure out where he came from and blast *him* to nowhere and back, we spotted the moon he was headed for.

I was preoccupied with the fighter at first and not thinking too much about the moon. I was ready to clear the distance between us and blast him off my list of troubles. All this happened real quick. There wasn't a lot of time to think about what the fighter was doing in the middle of nowhere.

But the moon . . . the old man called it. And before I could argue, I saw it was true. It wasn't a moon. It was a space station. The biggest space station you can imagine, the mother of space stations. It wasn't looking good. I thought I could turn us around and get us out of there, but we were caught in its tractor beam. The Death Star had us. If ever a space station was aptly named. . . .

I was ready to fight, but Ben pointed out the futility of that path. Sometimes my emotions get the best of me. That old man was quick. He had the mental agility of the best smugglers I've ever known. Before we were pulled inside the Death Star, he had us jettison some pods and change the ship's logs so that it looked like we had jumped ship. Smooth move. We stored ourselves in hidden compartments under the corridor floors. I knew being a smuggler would pay off big time one day. I guess you could say we were pretty valuable cargo. . . .

Sai'da: Why are you stopping, Mr. Solo? Does something trouble you?

Han: I don't want to reinvent history, but I saw this all a little differently in carbonite. Yeah, I was awake in a funny kind of way while I was amusing Jabba as a living sculpture. What was I titled, Chewbacca, "Handsome Man Grimacing"? Aw, forget it. There's no way I can make that little event amusing.

Anyway, even though I was hibernating, I had these dreams. Some seemed like actual dreams, but some of it seemed like real life with a twist.

Sai'da: What do you mean?

Han: I mean, when I first came out of carbonite I wasn't sure if I was still dreaming or if this was really happening. Too bad this isn't a dream.

When I was frozen, my dreams were sometimes episodes from real life. I would dream about when I was a kid or when I was with Bria Tharen. But then something odd would be in the dream that didn't occur in real life. It would make me realize I was dreaming.

I can't tell you how many times I had this realization.

In one dream I was in the cargo bay of the *Millennium Falcon* just like I was in real life. In reality and in the dream it was outer galaxy quiet. Deep quiet. Not a word from anyone. It was like I could feel that tractor beam locked onto my guts. In real life, I just kept waiting for the next sound to let me know what to expect. But in the dream version, I was looking at everyone very closely, like they couldn't see me.

I saw how Ben was moving calmly, with a clear purpose, like he knew what was about to unfold.

I saw how Luke would have followed that old man to the edge of the galaxy — the old man didn't even have to ask. There was something real pure in that. I know that sounds corny, but that's how I saw it.

And Chewbacca here, now don't go all soft on me, buddy, well, I saw how my life mighta been pretty lonely without him.

Chewbacca: Rrmph.

Han: Thanks for the hug, pal, but it's okay. I was appreciating you in the moment.

And the droids, of course. I know they've got their own personalities and quirks. But it was also as if they were reflections, on some level, of the people who owned them. As if they absorbed a moral code that wasn't even programmed into them — the integrity of the people around them. In this case, that was a good thing.

Now it's gonna get even weirder.

I'm gonna sound as crazy to you as the old man sounded to me when I met him.

Sai'da: Not at all. I find this unusually inter-esting, as I suspected I would. Please continue.

Han: I'm not sure I can explain. Why exactly is this so interesting to you anyway? What religion are you? I'm starting to have the feel-ing this isn't history, but some sort of confes-sion.

Sai'da: The B'omarr Order is not interested in confession, as it implies a moral judgment. We are interested in the mind. I am interested in the ways in which the changes in your think-ing have affected the changes in your actions. Do you see the difference?

Han: You don't mess around do you? You get right to the point. I'm starting to think you just might be a wise old monk, if you are old, but who knows? Your voice is so soft and calm I can't guess your age. Anyway, let me try again.

This is how it is: My brain might be playing in-tergalactic creature-chess with me, but . . .

Looking at the situation now, more or less dethawed from the little carbonite experiment, I think the things I realized in carbonite dream time were things that some part of my uncon-scious brain knew in real life. Like our time in the cargo hold. It's like the dream showed me what I could have known — if I would've just paid attention. Now, this ain't no Jedi Knight kind of thing, okay. This is just how it is for typ-ical human beings if we give it a chance. If we would listen to another part of ourselves. And that's it. I'm not saying any more.

Sai'da: I understand your insight, Mr. Solo. Perhaps the carbonite presented you with an unusual gift of self-awareness.

Han: I said I'm not saying any more.

Sai'da: Certainly. That's sufficient for now. Please return to your story, though, if you're ready.

Han: The story. Okay, you want it, you got it, ears, even though just talking about it makes me a little queasy.

It's like I'm seasick or something. You know how I got floating on the waves on Camus IV, pal, that time we tried to take a little vacation? Chewie and I on vacation — now there's something to laugh at. Anyway, that's how my stomach feels now. I can fly through space faster than almost anybody and feel just fine, but put me on a mild swell in an ocean and it's all over. You ever seen an ocean, Sai'da? Probably not, if you're stuck here on this wretched planet filled with sand and dust. . . .

You know, Tatooine invaded my hibernation dreams. I've spent a lot of time on this desolate planet, mostly hanging around Mos Eisley either waiting for jobs or payment. But I've also taken a landspeeder out quite a few times when boredom got the better of me. I've traveled around Tatooine enough to remember, in my bones somehow, the feeling of the heat and the dryness. Sometimes in my carbonite dreams I could see the entire surface of the planet just like when the *Falcon* is circling her, waiting for a landing port. It's a giant desert spotted with poor farmers' attempts to wrestle some moisture out of her. Only in my dream, it seemed pitiful. And it was like — here's the hibernation weirdness again — it was like something deep inside the planet was crying for water. It made me sad.

Sai'da: I welcome your sympathy with our planet. I often wish I could experience an environment other than this one. But we chose our fate and agree to the rules of it. So here I shall stay.

You look tired. Would you like to rest a moment before you continue?

Han: Yes. And maybe you could think about what it would be like to take a trip or two through the galaxy with me if I escape. Alter your fate a little, Sai'da. Think about it.

Han: Well, back to the Death Star. There was a lot of the old mayhem and subterfuge going on and a major new twist to disaster in the form of Her Worship. I've grown awfully fond of her these days, to put it mildly, but I can get irritated all over again just thinking about that first meeting.

Anyway, the plan the old man devised was a good starting point. As soon as the *Falcon* got sucked into the docking bay in the space station, they opened her up. I could hear the stormtroopers boarding her. You'd recognize the snap and click of their uniforms anywhere.

The Imperial troopers searched the ship and found just what they were supposed to find: the wrong information. As soon as they went to locate some heavy-duty scanners to make sure nobody was on board, we climbed out of our cramped hideaway. Let me tell you, those cargo bins are definitely better for spice than human beings.

Ben was barely out of hiding when he started talking about deactivating the tractor beam so we could escape. Even though I knew that's exactly what he would and should do, I called him a fool. He asked who was more foolish, "the fool or the fool who follows him?" I guess you know the answer to that one.

Things were moving fast again. As soon as we relieved the scanning crew of consciousness, Luke and I tricked a couple of stormtroopers to coming on board and borrowed their armor. You want to feel like a clown, try running around in that stiff white suit. I don't know how those guys can take themselves seriously. But Luke and I, looking all official now, led our mighty army off the ship and right into the sentry terminal.

Chewbacca: Naarghh. Narrowwl. Rawrrk.

Han: I know, I know. Chewie here disposed of the main sentry with a big Wookiee blow to the head, which cleared the way in. I wasn't trying to neglect your heroics, pal. I just keep getting ahead of myself.

Anyway, Artoo plugged into a computer outlet and located the main controls to the tractor beam. That little droid can take care of business in a hurry. Threepio was translating Artoo's beeps into a language we could understand — good old Basic.

Once the old man took in the information, he set out alone to dismantle the thing. Luke, being the kid he is, wanted to go. I was happy to stay behind, feeling that I'd paid my dues for this particular trip.

Ben reminded Luke that he had to deliver the droids safely to spare other planets the fate of Alderaan. That was my first clue that I should have been a little more observant of the droids. Ben said the kid's destiny was different from his. And then, very quietly he said, "The Force will be with you — always."

I guess if I'd been paying attention I would have figured out Ben knew he wasn't leaving that space station with us. Instead, I thought the old fossil had kind of lost his marbles — going off to face the Death Star alone.

Ben was gone, and the kid and I were having an argument about what to do next, when Artoo suddenly goes a little berserk. Threepio says that the droid has found her — Princess Leia. Now this was the first time I'd heard about any princess. Of course, Luke knew about her. He and the old man were hoarding more secrets than a smuggler hoards spice. But this princess was being held in a detention block and scheduled for termination, something neither of them knew.

Seemed the droids belonged to her. How she ended up on the Death Star was a whole other story. You can tell I entered late into this little conspiracy. I was fighting a whole war before I even knew what the blazes was going on.

Just the mention of the princess got Luke all worked up. He demanded I go marching off to the detention block with him to rescue the lady. But I wasn't keen on that suicide mission — until he mentioned she was rich, way rich.

You'd think I'd learn eventually that chasing after promises of vast amounts of wealth leads you nowhere. Especially when it comes from a gawky kid wanting to rescue a beautiful princess. . . . Does this sound like a fairy tale or what? Ha-ha. But I bought it, all right. I probably would have kissed a womp rat at that point if I thought it would have turned into a wealthy princess. Life is strange, I gotta tell you.

But what choice did I have? I don't mean to add what probably sounds like a petty concern to the tragedy of Alderaan, but my 15,000 credits were on the planet, too, you know. So off I went to save a damsel in distress. Or so I thought.

Now don't start thinking a sweet, soft, little bundle of female delight. And don't start thinking she's going to be thrilled to see us — her brave, handsome heroes. Boy, would you have *that* one wrong.

Sai'da: Is there something wrong, Mr. Solo?

Han: Of course there's something wrong, Sai'da. Leia is in the clutches of Jabba because she tried to rescue me. And I'm sitting here telling you stories while she's up there with that evil, disgusting — if he harms her in any way . . .

Chewbacca: Nrawwnk!!

Han: Okay, Chewie, okay. I'll sit down. I don't know where I thought I was going anyway. We both need to calm down, buddy.

I think maybe the historian here, once he gets the full scoop on our adventures, is going to be even more sympathetic to our predicament. Right, Sai'da?

Sai'da: I'm not sure what more I can say. I feel I have offered you all the assistance that I'm capable of at this time. We need to "play it by ear" I believe the expression is. Don't you think?

Han: Maybe. I guess it's our only choice for now. But just wait until I'm thinking more like Han Solo *before* carbonite. Then you're going to hear some ideas!

Sai'da: I believe you. And so, back to the Death Star and the recently discovered princess?

Han: Right.

So, now that the kid had me hooked on a rescue attempt, how do we get to the detention block? Believe it or not, Luke finally had a good idea — everybody has at least one, I figure. The plan was to make a fake prisoner out of Chewie. Chewbacca was a little grumpy about the restraints, but finally we were ready.

Off we went, leaving the droids to man our new command post, running on guts and a certain biped sophistication, if I do say so myself. Sometimes I gotta laugh just thinking of the stunts I pull to stay alive.

At the time it wasn't that funny. Talk about one uneasy trip through the innards of the Death Star. Even hidden inside those weird clown disguises we felt visible, like people could tell we didn't belong there. When you've been living the rough life, just the sight of all that shiny equipment and those sparkling metal corridors makes you nervous. Somebody forgot to tell me evil is clean.

Anyway, we finally arrived at the main detention center and reported in. Things started off all official-like and we thought we were pulling this thing off. Of course, all this gave way in a moment to general havoc when we sensed they weren't buying our little routine.

We were blasting guards and camera eyes and gate controls like we knew what we were doing. And in the chaos that followed we somehow managed to locate the princess.

Luke hightailed it to her cell while Chewie and

I tried to hold off some very unhappy Imperial troops. No, we didn't succeed. Like that's news.

Next thing you know Chewie and I were flying down the detention tunnel to warn the kid that the game was up. It was looking like we were cornered right near the royal one's cell.

Han: Now here's a touching moment, my meeting the princess. You know what her first words to me were? Do you? I'm talking gratitude, here. She glared at me and said, "Looks like you managed to cut off our only escape route." Like we had time to plan this little escapade for months! Then after she insulted our planning a little more, she blasted a grate in the wall next to me, almost frying me. No "I'm sorry," just a cute little "Somebody has to save our skins. Into the garbage chute, flyboy."

A piece of work, that one. Of course, now I admire her for taking charge like that. But at the time that attitude of hers was pretty hard to swallow. I mean, we'd just given her the only hope she had of keeping that royal skin of hers.

In all honesty, the garbage chute was probably our only escape route. Not that this fact impressed the furry one here. Oh, no, he took offense to the stench coming from the garbage. Fine time to find out something new about Chewbacca — he'd rather have blasters coming at him than offend his highly developed sense of smell.

Chewbacca: Warowwwrrk!

Han: Don't yell at me, pal, I'm just relating the facts. You gotta admit it's pretty funny. Though at the time I was ready to pluck your sensitive pelt, hair by hair.

If at all possible, Sai'da, avoid Imperial garbage. Besides the lovely perfume and the slimy water, there was some creature that kept trying to pull Luke to the depths of that pit for keeps. I was thinking, we risk all this and the kid is going to end up a tasty treat for some slime-sucking leech? We were all in a panic when the kid finally surfaced for good. Maybe he wasn't so tasty. I don't know.

We didn't have much time to consider Luke's good fortune, though. Next thing we knew the walls started closing in on us. The compressor had been activated.

That's when we first started to form into this ill-suited, but pretty hot fighting unit. Suddenly, we had to be working together. No one was a slacker, I've got to give them that. I like being with people who can keep their wits about them, use their heads in a crisis.

The problem is, when you're caught up in the

action, you don't notice you're starting to get sucked in.

Sai'da: In to what?

Han: Huh? Oh, you know, into this camaraderie thing. In this case, it led right to the Rebel enclave. When you're just reacting moment to moment, you don't have time to figure out what kind of bonds you're forming. I wasn't looking for involvement, believe me. My life's credo was always this: One man, one Wookiee command post. And I like it that way. My loyalties were to survival. Period.

Sai'da: I understand survival, but I'm curious about your lack of involvement.

Han: Actually, I'm curious about *your* lack of involvement. I still don't understand your deal — living here with Jabba the Hutt. How can you not be a part of his wayward circus, whether you want to be or not?

Sai'da: I have already explained that we are not associated with Jabba the Hutt.

Han: Oh, yeah, well, tell me how you can hang out in the same place with an immoral creature like Jabba and call yourself a monk? I know, you said you don't make moral judgments. Well, maybe you ought to. And you could start by taking Chewie and me to Leia. I think you could if you honestly wanted to. We could come up with a plan.

Sai'da: I cannot assist you with any such plan

now. I've explained why. Perhaps later . . . please, return to your history and speak to me of this woman you wished to rescue then as now.

Han: You might sympathize with me, Sai'da, but for a religious man, you sure don't seem to have much compassion.

I don't think I want to talk to you anymore.

Sai'da: You misjudge me, Mr. Solo. I know I don't express myself in the most compassionate manner, but I am not accustomed to discussions of this nature. Your frustration with your situation is understandable. What can I do, within my capacity, to prove to you my good intentions?

Han: Listen. I understand you're just one monk against Jabba's army, okay? I know the feeling. But you could at least get a map to us, couldn't you?

Sai'da: Yes, I believe that is something I could provide. Given time.

Han: And if I don't make it out of this little scrap alive, maybe you could look out for Leia or —

Chewbacca: Narowrrr!

Han: Let's be realistic, Chewie. It's a possibility. What do you say, compassionate one?

Sai'da: That seems a reasonable and decent request. I accept the responsibility to the best of my ability.

And now, if we are in agreement for a time, perhaps we could return to your history. Surely if I knew more about the princess it could only help me in my endeavors.

Han: You're right, I suppose. I just hope I can trust you. But since you seem to be my only option . . .

Let's see, why don't I describe how romance started to bloom right down there in the garbage unit. The compressor was about to mash us into particles for ejection into the vast garbage collector of space. Oh yeah, to be sure, we were about to say our last hallelujah, when those droids finally remembered to tune us in, and saved our sweet humanoid hides. That's when the princess started going all sweet on me. Yeah, that's my interpretation.

I have to admit she caught my attention. She's as pretty as any woman anywhere in the galaxy. And I should know. There are some planets that have a reputation for beautiful women, like Beckoning Call Starr 3. Well, I think they should put Alderaan at the top of the list.

Anyway, she had guts, too. Unfortunately, she also had a case of holding her royal nose too high in the sky. I don't mind telling you that I don't like taking orders from a woman. But I'm learning.

Besides, remember that woman I told you

about earlier — Bria Tharen — the one who pulled the blaster on me to keep me from my reward? Well, I'd rescued her, too, believe it or not. She was a slave I'd freed from the spice colony, Ylesia. Obviously, the romance did not end well. She was definitely an Alliance kind of woman only.

And I was sure Leia was a similar kind of trouble, maybe worse. You gotta wonder how much room a woman like that has in her heart for romance. And listen, you can't trust royal titles any more than you can trust a woman. To be sure.

The fact is, I trusted only my main pal and partner, Chewbacca. Huh, Chewie?

Chewbacca: Waurrgh.

Han: Actually, I rescued Chewie here, too. I never realized what a rescuing kind of guy I am. You talk long enough you start seeing things in a different light. Sight being relative at this point.

Yeah, I was actually in the Imperial starfleet before I turned to my alternative lifestyle. Me, a big career man.

The Imperials didn't care about Wookiee culture. Actually, they didn't care about much of anything except controlling the galaxy. But you probably know that by now. Anyway, Wookiees were a species enslaved under Imperial law. Can you believe that? There's a lot of slavery in the galaxy that people don't know about or choose to ignore. It's not just in the history books. It's happening right now. I tell you, people just don't know how to leave each other alone.

It can make you crazy watching the rotten stuff one species does to another. One day this slaver was particularly hard on one Wookiee, treating him so badly I couldn't stand by and watch. I'd heard the phrase, "It's none of your business," one too many times, so I took action.

My good deed was rewarded. I was court-martialed and booted from the majestic Imperial Navy. But here's the catch.

Chewbacca here was that Wookiee. And my intervention in his life, my making him my business, had established his "life debt" to me. Some Wookiee custom, that. He was ready to follow me anywhere, and he did. At first it annoyed the Corellian rats out of me that I couldn't ditch the furry beast.

Chewbacca: Bwaaark!?

Han: Easy, pal, you *know* that's how it was in the beginning. But it didn't take long for me to get to like having Chewie around. I mean, he was saving my life repeatedly once my new trade took off. Plus, he's good company if you understand the peculiarities of Wookiee talk. I sound pretty stupid trying to speak Wookiee, but I understand it well enough. Now we're friends. I don't like to think that a "life debt" is what keeps us partners anymore. It isn't, is it, Chewie?

Chewbacca: Naarghh.

Han: Thanks, buddy.

Han: Where was I? The garbage dump. Great place to return to. Yeah, the garbage compactor was putting the squeeze on us. Luke was trying to rouse Threepio on the comlink with no success. Finally I *wanted* to hear Threepio's voice and where was he? Anyway, we were pushing on the walls and using puny metal beams as braces like we had half a chance of stopping that giant machine. It was not a feel-good situation.

Suddenly, Threepio came squawking over the comlink and Luke shouted like a maniac to stop the compressors. We were a happy group there for a minute once Artoo stopped the walls from moving in on us. We were inches from a skinny death. A close call — again.

Leia used our brief celebration as an excuse to throw her arms around me. What could I do

but let her? Ha! I told you romance was bloom-
ing in the garbage dump.

Too bad we didn't have more time to enjoy
being alive before worrying about being killed
again.

That's about when the princess really started
working my nerves. She put aside our moment
of bonding in a hot second. She told me to do
as she said. I set her straight. I told her I only
took orders from one person, me! She said it
was a wonder I was still alive! Can you believe
this woman? Remember I told you, Sai'da, that
I don't like taking orders from women? Well,
especially that woman.

Facing Jabba the Hutt without any money
was sounding a lot better than sticking around
Her Worshipfulness for some huge reward.
Not that I had any choice at that point. Oh,
they'd suckered me into their little scheme all
right. So deep that the only way out was to
save all of us.

Ahhh, nuts. That's beside the point.

What was the point, anyway? Oh, great escape number 22, but who's counting? So, Luke
and I might have had a hard time maneuvering
in those Imperial get-ups, but it sure didn't stop
those troopers. They were on us the minute
we headed for the ship. Those guys had me so
worked up that I actually chased a whole pack

of them down the corridor single-handedly, screaming like a demented Wookiee —

Chewbacca: Vowraaark!

Han: No offense, pal, but you joined me, which proves that you actually *are* a demented Wookiee. Ha, ha, ha, ha!!!

Excuse our laugh attack, Sai'da. Just a moment's reprieve.

Well, our little wild foray after the stormtroopers gave Luke and Leia a chance to run for the *Falcon*. But the troopers suddenly figured out that a crazy man and a Wookiee weren't much of a match for a squad of heavily armed goons. Guess who was on the run then?

Chewie and I took quite a tour of the Death Star, making our way back to the docking bay. We figured there was no point leading them right to the *Falcon*.

The first wrong turn led us somewhere we definitely didn't belong. We were looking at enough spanking-new Imperial fighters to torment the entire galaxy. These guys knew how to run an Empire. Made my blood run cold just thinking what the Death Star could do. Chewbacca and I looked at each other and those ships, and I said, "If and when we reach the *Falcon*, we're outta here — with or without company!"

But Chewie kept telling me that they'd be there. I tried to remind him that he was being awfully concerned about someone who had called him a walking carpet.

"What about Luke and Ben?" you might ask. I mean, I'm not so sure I would have been able to leave them either, but I was willing to consider that solution.

We needed to get back to the docking bay, but at this point we were a little turned around. All right, we were lost. The Death Star is a maze. We made small forays down corridors that ended at locked doors. Things seemed unnaturally quiet after all the excitement we'd been through. It made us jumpy, hearing our footsteps echoing down hallway after hallway. I had to wonder, Where was everybody?

When we came to the next shut door Chewie was so frustrated he slammed his fist into it. Unbelievably, it opened. We looked at each other. Since no one was firing on us yet from the other side, we stepped in. What a trip! We were in the stormtroopers living quarters.

Chewie immediately throws me against the wall. But before I could protest, he points to a small camera attached to a metal arm extending from the far side of the ceiling. Just one — scanning the center of the room. The Imperials weren't even taking a chance on their own boys. I bet one nasty word about the Empire and you're jettisoned into space. It was a bad scene all the way around.

I said living quarters, but it was more like an insect colony. Shiny white beds were stacked ten high in rows covering a good portion of the room. Each bed had a monitor attached to it no bigger than my two fists. Every now and then some of them would flicker on and an announcement would be made. I wonder if those guys got any sleep what with the Empire keeping them informed all the time.

There was another door on the far side of the room, right below the camera. We slid along the walls, which were metal and cold to the touch, to the door. I put my hand on a place in the door that had a small indention, and the door opened. Looked like it was a storage area for all the stormtroopers' gear. One of the tall, podlike lockers was open, and a familiar white suit hung inside.

Chewie and I were wondering what to do next when we heard someone enter the living quarters. There was nothing to hide behind. We just had to hope that no one needed anything inside. We had our blasters ready, but I was not wanting to call attention to myself in that no-exit environment.

We weren't sure how many came in, but when they took off their helmets there were just two guys talking. It was an odd experience listening to them talk. I guess I thought they were going to have voices like droids and talk about the glories of the Empire or something. Instead, they were wondering when they got leave. One of them wanted to see his mother. The other guy just wanted a vacation someplace with trees.

It kind of flipped me out, to tell you the truth. I don't like seeing myself in my enemies, you know? That was one scary realization. I mean, they were just talking about regular stuff. Like me and Chewie would do. Do you get what I'm saying?

Sai'da: Yes. It would be easier if everyone were all good or all bad.

Han: Something like that. Not that they weren't the bad guys, because they were. I just wish they had been talking about evil instead of about their families and vacations. It would make life simpler, somehow. Still, once they've got their helmets on and are coming at you in swarms, I'm back to thinking of them as the insects of doom.

Anyway, we were listening to the troopers chatting and inching our way to the door. We didn't want to be caught too far inside the storage area in case they decided to check it out. Chewie rubbed past this wall unit of some sort and sparks started flying. The Death Star is not made to have organic material around, I can tell you that much.

It got quiet in the other room. I was pretty sure we were about to have a little face-to-face with the troopers. But then an announcement blasted into the living quarters that two intruders were cornered near the loading dock! "Everyone report to section five." That was not good news. Except for the fact that the troopers left in a hurry instead of investigating the noise Chewie instigated.

Chewie and I slinked out along the walls the same way we came in. We made our exit and had to decide: which gleaming corridor should we chose this time?

We were moving fast but stealth-like when we heard a strange hiss coming and turned into an alcove. Lucky us — we were just in time to see Darth Vader slither by. Now, I had heard tales of the Dark Lord over the years, but nothing prepared me for actually seeing him. I've seen some bad action in the galaxy, but this guy has everything beat. Have I mentioned that the Death Star was no place for a sane man? Well, this guy tipped the balance sheet. He was as evil as they get. I could see it. I could feel it. Catching his attention would not have been a smart move.

When we couldn't hear the hiss of Vader anymore, we wasted no time heading back to the docking bay. I was finally getting oriented.

Still, we managed to pick up and lose a few more troopers on our way. I quickly forgot my insight into the inner lives of the stormtroopers when they opened fire on us. They weren't like me. They were in the same ugly game as Darth Vader.

Vader might be the walking embodiment of evil, but even evil needs help. So every trooper we downed with our blasters, I thought of as another speck of evil eliminated.

We finally wrapped up our tour of the Death Star, and arrived back at the landing pad.

The *Falcon* was waiting for us, guarded by the ever-loyal boys in white. She'd never looked more beautiful to me.

Luke and Leia came running up behind us. I was glad to see them, too, of course, but I did wonder what took them so long.

We were all just staring at the *Falcon*, waiting to make a move. Have you noticed that advance planning is not our strong point?

Suddenly, the troopers noticed a commotion and moved away from my ship, giving us a shot at boarding her. We were hightailing it toward our one chance out of the Death Star when Luke spotted Ben. You'll never guess what he was doing. Dueling with Darth Vader! What a sight that was, two guys who couldn't be more different, Ben and Vader, fighting with their antique lightsabers.

Then it got even stranger. . . .

The old man spotted Luke. Now, I didn't see this so clearly, but Luke did, poor kid. And I trust him on this. Ben apparently just raised his lightsaber in front of his face, stood still, and let Vader take him out.

Had to be a sacrifice. It freaked the kid completely and he screamed, "Nooooo!"

That got the troopers' attention. They started firing on him and the kid was so mad or stunned or something that he just stood there firing back. I was trying to cover him some, but it wasn't easy. It's never easy when firepower is coming your way, and don't let anybody tell you different. I finally got the kid's attention and shouted to him to blast the door shut. He did. That trapped Vader on the other side and kept more of the Imperial insects from joining the fray.

We had made our way over to the *Falcon* when Luke finally recovered enough to get himself into the ship. The droids were already inside. At least they know how to take care of themselves. I guess we all did. Because now we were back together and ready for the ultimate test.

Han: This was it. The moment of truth. Did the old man get the tractor beam out of commission? The thought of making a grand exit only to be snared again wasn't exactly appealing.

No problem. We were out of that docking bay and into free, glorious space faster than you could say, "Old man, you were one crazy antique, but you knew what you were doing."

Well, not quite free space. We still had to earn that. The sentry ships had us spotted and those TIE fighters were moving in on us. It's lucky you don't have much time to think about it while it's happening or you could get real depressed.

I was worried about the kid being able to help. He looked so stunned after watching the old man go down. But he came back fast. He's a lost child, sometimes, Luke is, but he always manages to come through. He's got guts and he learns quick. It's a natural fighter's skill. He took to the *Falcon*'s defense system quicker than an asteroid flash. Held his own, too. You should have heard him when he took down his first ship.

Well, aren't I sounding like the proud papa?

Anyway, I didn't do too bad either. Luke and I were swinging around in those gunner seats, honing in on the planes like we were playing Cockpit Daredevils back on Mos Eisley. There's a game for you. Only the stakes were a little higher in this showdown.

We took care of those TIE fighters better than any ace right out of the Academy. Chewbacca and the princess were holding down things in the cockpit. Seems Chewie melted a little when the princess gave him a big hug. He immediately forgot the walking carpet comment.

Chewbacca: Narowrrr!

Han: Come on, buddy, I'm not making fun of you. The princess works her charms on all of us. You gotta watch that stuff, is all.

Anyway, we fixed the problem standing between us and hyperspace and made the jump. Man, that's a great feeling to go reeling into hyperspace and know no Imperial goon is gonna be able to follow. Smooth. Easy.

Too easy, the princess informed us. She was

sure they let us go, that being the only reason for our escape. Now that got me. Once again I've rescued her, and she's saying it was too easy. That they were tracking us.

Ever notice how mad you get when you suspect someone is right and you don't want them to be? She's a smart number, that girl, and . . . hmmm . . .

Sai'da: Are you tired again, Mr. Solo? Do you wish to rest?

Han: No. I was just thinking.

Sai'da: Please share your thoughts, if possible. I am not just interested in what happens to you, per se. I am curious about how you interpret events, how you develop bonds with your comrades. The changes in your emotional state are intriguing.

Han: Intriguing, huh? You're a piece of work, Sai'da, the way you talk. But I guess that's one way of looking at it.

Actually, I was just thinking of the old man. I guess he knew all along it was his last mission. It sure was hard on the kid, though. I mean, Luke lost not only his Jedi mentor, but a father figure, too. He was pretty much alone in the galaxy now. He seemed even younger to me then. I had this impulse to take care of him, but I got a hold of it. 'Cause that was the *last* thing I needed, a kid brother to worry about.

I had enough worries. I had to deliver this

group to the Rebel base on the fourth moon of Yavin in order to collect my money so I could pay off Jabba. You're not a free man when you've got bounty hunters sniffing your trail. I tried to explain this to Leia, but she wasn't hearing any of it.

It was about then I learned what the little droid was hiding — plans for the Death Star. All this time and I still didn't know exactly what we were doing until Leia finally saw fit to inform me. Yeah, I never would have guessed Artoo was wanted by the entire Galactic Empire.

Up until then you'd have thought I was the enemy. And suddenly Leia was shocked that I wasn't taking on her revolution or just dying to protect her until doomsday. She even seemed surprised that I actually wanted the reward I'd earned.

She said to me, "If money is all that you love, then that's what you'll receive." Which is kind of a crummy way to put it, if you ask me. Of course I cared about the money!! That's why I was hired in the first place!

Listen, I'm no wealthy prince. The easy life is not something I know anything about. Maybe money doesn't matter to some people, but if you're always scrambling to survive, it means something. Something big. Especially if, without it, Jabba the Hutt is going to end any chance you have of retirement.

Luke was enjoying the situation, I think. It made him look good. He started expressing how much he cared about things other than money. And Leia liked that attitude. You bet she did.

Those two were getting under my skin like nobody else ever had.

And Chewie didn't help matters any. We had a heart-to-heart on the way to Yavin. He said he wanted to join forces with the Alliance and help save the galaxy. Can you believe this? He was sounding noble. Sounding more loyal to a couple of strangers than to me.

Chewbacca: Aroaw!

Han: I know, I know. I'd just never heard Chewbacca disagree with me before. He actually wanted me to forget about the money and help the Rebels. Forget about the money. Right. I told him that we had to save ourselves first. Not to mention the fact that fighting the Imperial forces, especially after seeing the Death Star, seemed like a job for a fool. I'm not real big on lost causes, mister, like you must be. You get a kick out of sitting here getting me to tell you my last stories before my time runs out? Yeah, you think I'm fascinating. Well, let me tell you, I'm no laboratory experiment. You understand?

Sai'da: Oh, dear. I thought we *had* reached

an understanding, Mr. Solo. I have offered you my limited assistance. You are offering me knowledge of history that will influence the galaxy. You are offering me insight into the ways in which individual lives and choices affect this history. I no longer know how to explain my intent.

Han: I know your intent, Sai'da, I really do. But let me be perfectly honest, okay? Here's the deal: As much as I'm enjoying hearing myself talk, what I'm really after is a little more information from you. As I said, maybe I can trust you. I'm starting to think so. But time's passing and I still don't know what's happened to Leia. I'm not thinking her chances are much better than mine of surviving this demented resort. So, now it's your turn again: Could you just tell me exactly where Leia is?

Sai'da: Give me a moment, please, to meditate.

Han: Meditate? Fine. Whatever hocus-pocus you've got, use it.

Sai'da: She is with Jabba, not locked away like you. That is all I know.

Han: Is that supposed to be good news? Let me tell you, being a beautiful woman is no protection from Jabba's temper. I couldn't exactly see or hear what was going on while I was in carbonite, but sometimes a Jabba moment would penetrate my little dream world. None of the moments were good and most of them were violent.

Sai'da: Mr. Solo, let's go over this again. Even if we were to go to Leia, how do you propose to rescue her? I am not accustomed to such attempts, but it seems to me a blind man, a Wookiee, and a monk would be no match for Jabba's armed men. And I am opposed to violence in any case. Remember, I have agreed to secure a map for you.

Han: I wasn't asking for armed support, my friend. Maybe I was just exploring my emotional life. The longer I sit here and the stronger I feel, the angrier I get. I don't know what to do when I can't take action.

It's hard to believe that talking is the only thing that's going to help me, but maybe it is.

Just give me a minute, okay?

Where was I, anyway?

Sai'da: I believe you were discussing your disagreement with Chewbacca over his desire to assist the Rebels.

Han: All right. Not that I like talking about our first real argument.

Chewbacca: Rarrghhh!

Han: Don't get all apologetic on me, pal. You had your point of view and, as we both know, it turned out to be a good one. It was just a rough place to be, zipping through space, feeling alone, staring out at the long, dark tunnel of time. Whoa. I'm getting too poetic for my own good.

All this talk is going to turn me from a fighter into a philosopher if I don't watch it.

So anyway, Chewie and I disagreed. I don't think I'd ever heard my pal quite so eloquent. He was talking about the Wookiee code. How we'd saved each other. And that meant we were obligated to each other and some such thing. Chewie was emotional. Loyalty kept coming up.

And seeing Darth Vader had thrown him for a loop, too. He was taking sides with the good guys. I mean, he was thinking the Rebels probably didn't believe in slavery. Good guess, actually.

You think you know a person. I thought Chewbacca was low key and just along for the ride. And then he gives this lecture on Wookiee theology. It blew my mind, to tell the truth.

Finally Chewie just sat there quietly looking at his big Wookiee feet like he didn't even know me. I couldn't convince him to agree with me. I knew he would stick with me, but that's different from seeing my point of view. I didn't like my main pal being unhappy with me.

I kept thinking of things I didn't want to think about.

Sai'da: For example?

Han: You like hearing about the hard stuff, don't you?

Well, I was mostly thinking about the kid and the princess. They were both equal parts torment and, well, something a lot nicer. And about the old man dying like he did, sacrificing his life for a reason I didn't comprehend. Everything was starting to bother me: the Imperial forces, Darth Vader. Something was closing in on me and I didn't like it one bit.

And my best buddy was no help at all. He just made it worse by sitting there like some silent judge. Like he pitied me.

Sai'da: What was closing in on you?

Han: A feeling of no escape!

I'm not used to making decisions about anybody but me. It works better that way. Or it used to. I told you I'm not an introspective kind of guy. And when I am, as you've noticed, it tends to upset me. I prefer action.

Sai'da: You've seen a lot of action in the galaxy, Mr. Solo. It's strange, isn't it? I am accustomed to inactivity and thinking. My life would be very difficult for you. And conversely, even the thought of as much action as you have accomplished makes me quite nervous.

Han: Yeah, but here we are locked up together anyway. And I'm the one having to do all the thinking and talking. Kind of a bad deal, if you ask me.

Sai'da: And I am the one responsible for smuggling notes and securing you a map. I, too, am out of my element.

Han: Weird, huh. I guess we're having an influence on each other whether we like it or not.

Sai'da: Yes. I believe this will be my first real adventure.

Han: And this is definitely my first recorded history. What are you using anyway?

Sai'da: A data pad. I believe I am the only monk in my order to have one. A gift. But that is another story.

Shall we return to the Han Solo story again?

Han: Sure. If I can't create any action around here, I might as well be talking about when I could.

Han: We brought the *Falcon* down on the moon on the far side of Yavin. It was a welcome sight. Something about all the green and trees made you feel you might be human again. Ever notice that the smell of a forest is an antidote to pretty much anything that ails you? I guess not, stuck here on Tatooine, the dustbin of the galaxy.

Anyway, the Rebel base was a huge stone temple cut into this massive green, jungle land-scape. It was pretty impressive for a makeshift operation. I wasn't expecting such high-class technology in the middle of nowhere.

You know what else surprised me? That the Rebels were so numerous. They must have been recruiting all over the galaxy. Last time I heard, there were just bands of them here and there. They were supposedly more about mak-ing a point than actually threatening anyone.

Not that this bunch was exactly a match for the Death Star. But then, nothing was a match for that thing.

The base was like a giant insect hive with people running around and preparing for action.

As soon as we got to the base, the Commander and Leia started to talk. He tried to express his worry. I mean, Alderaan had been blown to nowhere, and he was fearing the worst. But she wasn't having any of it.

You know, maybe this sounds self-absorbed — no surprise — but it just hadn't occurred to me that Leia had lost her home. Worse, she'd watched it be destroyed. But she didn't want to talk about it with the Commander. She just wanted to get on with the struggle against the Empire.

I'll tell you, it takes guts to keep going when you've lost practically everything. She wasn't looking for any sympathy or expecting special treatment. She didn't shed a tear. I kept looking at her. I was impressed. Okay, more than that. It made me feel, ahhh, you know, tender toward her.

I was a regular battle station of emotions about that woman. Luke, too, for that matter. I never worked so hard to not like two people in my life.

I just wanted to be me again. Get my money.

Pay Jabba. Find some work. Not worry about anybody or anything. And I tried. You can't say I didn't try.

We'd barely said our sweet hellos before they had Artoo plugged into the main computer to download the Death Star's technical read-outs. It didn't look good. The Death Star had a defensive system that looked invincible.

Nothing was looking good except my reward. It turns out they didn't have much to pay me with except precious metal. And they didn't want to part with that, I can tell you. But they kept their word.

I think there were those in the Alliance who wanted to send us packing empty-handed. But Luke and Leia knew how to honor their word, at least. I could get good profit out of that metal. Plus, I figured they wouldn't be needing it once the Death Star arrived. I had a grim outlook on the Rebels' destiny. I wanted out quick.

Luke wasn't about to give up on me though. I guess he figured we'd continue our happy little family unit. He wanted me to be a hero. He still hadn't figured out that I wasn't fighting for some big cause; I was fighting for me and Chewbacca.

Luke followed me to the washroom and spoke Ben's name like it had supernatural power or something. How Ben thought there was more to me than I wanted to admit. Like that was going to impress me so much I'd say, "Oh, wonderful, now I'll be a fool like the rest of you and sit here and wait for the end of the world as I know it." Right.

You know, Sai'da, this wasn't about courage. I've got enough guts for twenty guys. And that's not bragging. I've proved my stuff. I wasn't about to take up a cause I hadn't chosen and do something stupid. You don't plop yourself in front of a blaster unarmed, if you know what I mean. Even a fool knows there's a difference between courage and suicide.

Now, Luke, all he could think about was causes and courage. He'd gone and volunteered to be a pilot. A pilot. The kid was barely off the farm! And the Alliance was willing to give him a plane and a ticket to oblivion. And he wanted me to join him. Flattered me with how they needed good, experienced pilots. Oh, I'm good all right. But I'm smart, too.

When he started talking to me about giving my life some meaning, I went for my reward and my life. Luke's about to be blown to the outer reaches of the galaxy and he's wanting to discuss the meaning of life. Give me a break.

Well, I didn't get much of a break because here comes the princess. She doesn't give you much of a chance to keep feeling tender toward her. I'd had my discussion with the kid, so I kept it short with her. I just said, "No," to every plea and insult.

I did add that maybe she could do Luke a favor and keep him from dying a young death. I knew she was the only one who could keep him grounded. But what was the difference, really? That would be just as dangerous. It was just a matter of choosing how to go — by land or by air. There was no stopping the Death Star.

Chewbacca managed to keep his thoughts to himself.

Chewbacca: Bowraakk!

Han: I know, Chewie, it was hard to disagree with me and keep it to yourself. And you were trying to stand by me — in a very subdued kind of way.

I was curious though about what kind of cross-eyed plan they would come up with to attack the space station. So, I sat in on the briefing. At first, I couldn't believe what I was hearing.

This guy, Dodonna, said the only way to destroy the Death Star was to send small one-man fighters in. That the Imperials were prepared for a full frontal assault, but not the one-man jobs. That was their only weakness. Maybe a fighter could penetrate their defense.

Actually, when I thought about it, the plan made some sense to me. You know how you're all preoccupied with the big thing in front of you and then something little comes along and knocks you for a loop? It's always about what you don't see coming.

So, there they were, all these misfit Rebels, suited up and intent, listening to Dodonna's one-chance scenario. They would have to approach this monstrous orb in their midget fighters. They would have to skim along a narrow trench on the surface in search of a two-meter-wide exhaust port. And, at high speed, drop a proton torpedo down it.

Ultimately, I wasn't buying it.

Those pilots were ready to do their duty, but they looked stunned, like they knew it was an impossible task. There was no small amount of grumbling. Except Luke, who was bragging about bull's-eyeing womp rats on Tatooine. Yeah, this was going to be some fun summer day just like back on the farm. I'm tellin' you, the kid thinks he's invincible.

Anyway, Leia was right about the Imperial forces having us tagged. They tracked us to Yavin and were moving in for their final day of glory — the destruction of the Rebellion. Not that I wanted to think too much about it.

Chewie and I went back to load up the *Millennium Falcon* with the reward that was going to save *us* from oblivion. Luke came by to harass me one more time. Sure, I was feeling pretty weird about seeing him off to his death and me doing nothing about it. But I didn't let on that anything was on my mind. My smart mouth kept working despite my conflict.

I offered to let him come with me. I said I could use a good fighter. Which seemed to disgust him even more. He finally left, but not before I found myself saying, and of all things, meaning it: "May the Force be with you." It just kind of popped out. I don't know. Luke had that warrior's glow you read about in the ancient histories. It made me want to say something decent to him.

Then Chewie starts in with his looks again. He wasn't going to let up on me yet. Money right there in his hands and he's ready to walk away from it. A Chewie I'd never seen before.

Actually, I wasn't exactly myself either. It was like I was two people with different ideas about what to do. The old me that knew how to take care of myself was having an argument with some new guy who wanted to be a hero or something.

So, I ended this conversation I was having with myself and started watching all these kids and ragtag pilots climbing into their fighters. They were ready for their suicide mission, pumped up. Even Artoo looked excited being plopped into the back of Luke's X-wing. His buddy Threepio was trying to stay calm and be of some use to the princess. I was so keyed up

I was imagining an emotional life for the droids. You can't help but do that sometimes.

It's funny how there's never a right way to say good-bye to people.

I was hanging back like some shadow creature so Leia couldn't give me her princess stare. But I was watching and listening to the beginning of the attack on the Death Star. I was imagining the shock of our pilots when they first spotted that enormous space station.

Listening to the incoming reports of Rebel ships being destroyed really shook me up. I knew Luke was out there watching his new pals being blown into nothing and still moving forward, waiting for his big chance. I could just see him and Artoo, courageous as ever, barreling around the Death Star.

It seemed like I could see the whole thing unfolding. Maybe it's from being a pilot or from always being on the run, but I could sense where everyone was. Not just that, it was like I knew when a guy would make his next move. My mind turned into this giant computer grid.

I was going half crazy just sitting there. Not doing anything. So I left. What was the point in sticking around for the obvious conclusion?

I didn't want to see Leia trying to be brave. I knew that every time a ship was destroyed, it would take a little light out of her. You know how someone seems a little less human when they lose people they love? A little more like a zombie?

Ahhh, anyway, it made my heart hurt just to look at her. She and Luke already seemed like they had known each other forever. I couldn't imagine what was going to happen when he went down.

Not to mention the countdown was on. Everybody was listening to this dismembered voice, "Death Star approaching. Estimated time for firing range, fifteen minutes." How handy to know beforehand when you're going to be annihilated. I was out of there.

Han: Chewie and I had the *Falcon* loaded. We boarded her without saying much. I was too busy talking to myself again.

We blasted off. I'd made it. I had the money to pay off Jabba. The Imperials were too busy to pay any attention to the *Falcon*'s exit. I had a clear ride ahead of me.

So what was the problem? I should have been feeling great. A free man again. But I couldn't help myself. I had to monitor the battle going on back at the Death Star. Chewie and I were silently taking in the destruction of the Rebel pilots. Those boys were going at their mission with everything they had. They were standing tall against the Imperial forces and their TIE fighters. It really got to me.

It was tough going for the Rebel pilots — either they couldn't get near the opening to shoot the big one down the shaft, or they couldn't hit a target that small once they did. They were covering for each other at extreme risk. I couldn't even keep track of how many pilots had gone down. It was last-chance time when they gave the word to Luke.

Suddenly, I knew we were heading the wrong way. We turned the *Falcon* around and torked at maximum speed to the Death Star.

Three new TIE fighters had entered the fray. I had a bad feeling about those guys. Time was running out and it was up to the kid to pull off a miracle. They were closing in on him. I figured if there was going to be one last fight, at least it was going to be a fair one.

Luke was down there skimming along the trench in his X-wing with his computer turned off, ready to blast one down the chute by eyeballing it — if he could get the chance. Well, I was there to give him that chance. Those TIE boys didn't see me coming. See, there's an advantage to entering the game late: The element of surprise.

Sai'da: So you entered the battle for Luke?

Han: Kind of. But more than that. I couldn't take it anymore. I didn't want those Imperial TIEs humming down passageways behind any of our boys. They're an evil-looking bunch, the Imperial forces, including their ships. Even after all the casualties and failed attempts, each Rebel was willing to give his life for Luke's chance to blow the Death Star out of the galaxy. That kind of bravery gets to you. I knew I had to help the kid. And at that moment I knew in my gut that I was with the Rebel Alliance. It's like it all becomes clear. And when you know something that sure inside of you, your body just takes off and all you can do is follow. I was going to make sure that Darth Vader — and don't ask me how I knew it was him — didn't ruin the kid's chance.

I told you I like action. Coming at those Imperial TIEs and giving them the surprise of their lives was pretty wild. The Death Star was seconds from eliminating the Rebel base. Talk about changing the course of history for the galaxy. That would have been a grim story for you.

But it didn't happen. First I blasted one of the wingmen. A clear shot. He didn't know what hit him. That got the attention of the other two. There was no time for subtle games or maneuvers. I just came right at those TIE fighters. Scared the one guy into making a move that slammed him against the wall of the trench. But not before he'd nicked Darth Vader's wing and sent him spinning out of control into space.

I think getting to say, "You're all clear, kid," to Luke was one of the high points of my life.

And the kid. I still can't believe it. Luke

dropped those proton torpedoes down the chute and made something beautiful out of evil. The Death Star exploded into a star field like nothing you've ever seen. What are the chances of hitting a shot like that? One in a million! Amazing. The kid really showed his stuff.

DATA PAD ENTRY 14

Sai'da: How were you feeling about yourself once you joined in the battle?

Han: Thrilled. When the Death Star exploded and the reality of the situation hit — that was something. Flying the *Falcon* back to the base with the other Rebels, thinking about what we had just done . . . I mean, it was unbelievable. This scrappy little group of Rebels had taken down the biggest space station in history!

I wasn't used to being a part of the good guy team, if you know what I mean. Outwitting the Imperial forces with a smuggled load is one thing. But going up against them was something else. And not for any reward, but because it was the right thing to do.

Most of the excitement was from the simple high of battle, but part of it was from belonging to something bigger than myself. When you're working together with people you believe in, your world suddenly seems a little bigger. It's a rush. For a while anyway.

Instead of turning the *Falcon* around and jumping into hyperspace like I normally would have, I followed the boys back to base.

Yeah, we were a wild bunch of pilots. We felt alive. We couldn't say enough nice things about each other. I was even proud of the little R2 unit. I was thinking of him as wounded in battle! And Threepio was so beside himself with worry over Artoo that he offered to donate his circuits to him. We were all crazy in the way that being happy can make you sometimes. I was hugging Luke and Leia. Chewie and I were cheering and embracing like long-lost brothers.

All the Rebel forces were yelling for us once we got back, and it seemed like we were a big, happy, friendly family.

Eventually things calmed down, though. I got ahold of myself. Then doubt crept in again, like, what do I think I'm doing hanging out here with these people? I've got debts to pay and a life to live. I can't go chasing around the galaxy like some hero with a fairy princess and her noble knight.

Han: Odd. Now here I am, the big hero, locked up and helpless while the fairy princess is held captive. Great fairy tale. And where is the noble knight?

Chewbacca: Bwaarrk!

Han: You think so, Chewie? Well, I hope you're right about Luke. I've got to admit that just remembering how he took the Death Star gives me hope. Last minute saves. That's something Luke and I have in common.

Sai'da: It seems you have much in common.

Han: You've got to be kidding!

Sai'da: It's true that I don't know Luke, but it certainly seems your fates are interlinked.

Han: Can't deny that.

Sai'da: Yes, and it appears that the explosion of the Death Star didn't end your association. I thought you wished to return to Tatooine with the money for Jabba the Hutt. Considering your current circumstances, something must have detained you. Your newfound affection for . . .

Han: No!

Chewbacca: Vrowk-rr-vorghh.

Han: True, one thing leads to another, and maybe if we *had* left before the ceremony, things would have turned out different. But the ceremony itself is not important, Chewie.

Sai'da: A ceremony? I believe the ritual of ceremony for any given culture is of interest.

Han: You would.

Chewbacca: Rruumpph!

Han: Okay, pal.

I don't really want to talk about the ceremony, Sai'da, but since Chewbacca wants to hear about it again for some peculiar Wookiee reason, I guess you're in luck.

To begin with, I had my doubts about the ceremony. It was a little too formal for my taste. Plus, I didn't like all the show. And I was pretty eager to get back to Tatooine. But everybody, especially Leia, wanted to honor me.

I didn't know what to do. I didn't want anyone to have to beg me. I mean, they're good people and how could I turn away from them? But I needed some time alone.

There was too much excitement. I thought if I could just think things through, I could figure out my life a little.

Luke showed up first. What a great kid, when you get right down to it. He was so happy. He kept saying he knew I would join the fight and not let him down. How an ace pilot like me deserved a ceremony.

It was like I was his new best friend. His sincerity embarrassed me a little. That kid has a feeling and he just shows it, you know? The ceremony thing was made for guys like him. I told him I'd consider it after he'd hugged me for about the tenth time.

"Ben would have wanted it," Luke said. "He would have been proud. I know he's proud. I know he knows."

The kid was starting to sound like the old man. He was even getting that look in his eye.

Then the commander came to see me. I was honored. And he said *he* would be honored if I would stay for the ceremony. Everyone was being so nice to me that I was starting to feel a little shy. Which for me is a new way of being. I mean, everyone was a hero in this battle, so why was I getting the medal?

But it was Leia who really got to me. She talked about all the guys who didn't make it back to the base, all those brave kids. She said how she wished they could be there for the ceremony. It would mean something to them. And if it didn't mean anything to me, then think of the pilots who died for the Alliance and for one another. At least I could honor them.

She was right. I couldn't turn my back on what they had died for and just say, "Oh, no thanks, I'm taking my reward and heading home."

It was such a small thing she was asking me to do. And yet it was a big thing, honoring those who had made the ultimate sacrifice.

I said yes.

She was so gentle. And beautiful. Once she had accomplished her mission, she had a chance to rest. It looked good on her. Even her voice seemed softer.

Chewie was thrilled. He had wanted to stay all along.

DATA PAD ENTRY 16

Han: Now that everybody was in agreement about the ceremony, all we had to do was show up. Luke, Chewie, and I were dressed in our finest, which wasn't much, and waiting for the big deal.

Suddenly the door zoomed open and there we were. Rebels were lined up in formation like they were the leaders of the entire Galactic Empire. There was an aisle for us to walk down. So off we went, Luke and I in the front, followed by Chewbacca, who was so excited he was howling his best Wookiee howl.

Luke and I were a little more contained. At least on the outside.

I have to tell you, though, once I got over how stupid I felt, it was a thrill parading down that tarmac to the stage with all those troops lined up in respect for us.

It was a thrill, wasn't it, buddy? A big-time deal.

Chewbacca: Arrorrkkk!

Han: We looked out at all these Rebels standing tall and we were a part of them. Being respected by honorable men and women is not something I'd experienced a lot of in my life.

Okay. It got to me, all right? I was happy for a while there.

The princess was in a charming mood, too. She slipped the medal over my head and smiled. No wise comments. I winked at her so she'd know I understood she was crazy about me. No, I was just feeling good. Not much you can actually say at a time like that.

And Luke, the kid looked so happy and proud I was about ready to adopt him.

Even the droids seemed happy. Artoo was beeping away and Threepio was patting him on the head. I'm thinking they actually do have more emotion than we give them credit for. Heck, I'm thinking I have more emotion than I give myself credit for.

That ceremony was one time we were all in agreement. No arguing over what to do or who was right or where the money was or who was giving orders. Just all of us feeling good that things had turned out right. We'd each done our job in the way we knew how. Life's usually a little more complicated than that, trust me.

Once the ceremony was over we were back to making decisions about the rest of our lives. Back to being just ordinary human beings. For better or worse.

Sai'da: But didn't the ceremony change you in some way?

Han: I don't know. Maybe it did. Once I was treated with that kind of respect, I started looking at myself in a different way. Wondering who I could be, not just how I could make the next cash transaction.

Not that I figured it all out right then and there. I still haven't, actually. I mean, look where all that reflection got me, Sai'da — sitting blind in this damp, cold cell waiting for that filthy, oozing creature that's got Leia to come kill me.

It always comes back to that, doesn't it?

Han: I'm still worried about Leia. I need to stretch instead of sitting on this cold, wet bench. That's better. Don't let me walk into a wall, Chewie.

Do they ever feed you in this nightmare? I mean, I haven't had a meal in a year now. I'm starting to think I might be hungry.

Sai'da: I'm not aware of their meal schedule for prisoners. But I don't think they are terribly concerned about your well-being.

Han: No kidding. Have you ever considered they might not let *you* out of here? Of course, how different can this be from the monk's life?

Sai'da: Oh, very different. To be deprived of my books would be unthinkable.

Han: You know, I understand your interest in history. I really do. I'm not without a certain interest myself. But sometimes don't you want to actually be out and *living* life, making some history of your own?

Sai'da: It is a desire I try to contain. It is not considered a proper concern in my order.

Han: Sure, but that doesn't change the desire, does it? I mean, let's say I get out of here with a little assistance from you. Wouldn't you like to take a look at some of those places you read about? Maybe see a few ancient scrolls? Walk through a temple of unknown origin?

Sai'da: You do those things?

Han: You'd be surprised at the interesting situations you get into as a smuggler. It's not all a matter of life or death. Tell me you wouldn't like to take a cruise around the galaxy on the *Millennium Falcon*.

Sai'da: Well, certainly, I understand the appeal. Although it is heresy for me to even admit that. But I am, after all, human. Far too human to be worthy of the B'omarr Order, I fear.

Han: We've all got our inner battles, it seems. One thing about being in carbonite, I realize situations are a lot more complex than even I figured.

Chewbacca: Waarrk!

Han: Chewie says he hears someone coming. You expecting the guard?

Sai'da: No. I would not think so soon.

Han: Listen, my friend, whatever happens,

don't forget the deal we made. I can trust you, right?

Sai'da: Yes. Most assuredly.

Han: Chewie, who is it? Did Sai'da leave?

Chewbacca: Arroarwwk!

Han: Boba Fett?

Sai'da: I will return . . .

Han: I was just saying the smell couldn't get any worse in here. And you show up, Fett, and make a liar out of me. So, what brings a rat like you down —

DATA PAD ENTRY 18

Sai'da: My conversation with Han Solo has come to a halt — a temporary one, I hope. But there is no telling what Boba Fett, the most notorious bounty hunter in the galaxy, will do to him.

I am standing outside the doorway of Han's cell, unable to move. A strange feeling has come over me. I am a religious man, a man of compassion in spirit and words — but not in action. I cannot prevent the death of Han Solo. I am no match for a bounty hunter. And never before has this been a source of frustration!

Mr. Solo has given me a lot to think about. The virtues of bravery and action. Loyalty and comradeship. Humor.

I walk away from Han Solo's cell now. But

only to get a glimpse of his princess. Perhaps I had better learn some of the ways of Mr. Solo, if I am to protect her.

Until then, I pray for the continuation of Han Solo's history. . . .

ENTER THE STAR WARS INTERGALACTIC CONTEST!

Win a Poster that Really Glows in the Dark!

500 winners! Purchase required.

For a chance to win a Star Wars galaxy poster, buy all three Star Wars Journals and answer the essay question below.

Official Rules: 1. To enter, complete this official entry form or hand print your name, address, birthdate, and telephone number on a 3" x 5" card, answer essay question on separate piece of paper in 100 words or less, and mail together with register receipt(s) verifying the purchase of all three books (*The Fight For Justice* by Luke Skywalker, *Hero For Hire* by Han Solo, and *Captive to Evil* by Princess Leia Organa) to: Star Wars Galaxy Poster Contest, c/o Scholastic Inc., P. O. Box 7500, Jefferson City, MO 65102. Enter as often as you wish, one entry to an envelope. All entries must be postmarked by 8/15/98. Partially completed entries or mechanically reproduced entries will not be accepted. Sponsors assume no responsibility for lost, misdirected, damaged, stolen, postage-due, illegible or late entries. All entries become the property of the sponsor and will not be returned. 2. Contest open to residents of the USA (except residents of Vermont and North Dakota) no older than 15 as of 8/15/98, except employees of Scholastic Inc., its respective affiliates, subsidiaries, advertising, promotion, and fulfillment agencies, and the immediate families of each. Contest is void where prohibited by law. 3. Winners will be judged by Scholastic Inc., whose decisions are final, based on their answer to the subjective question. 500 winners will be chosen. Only one prize per winner. All prizes will be awarded before 10/30/98, depending on the number of entries received. Except where prohibited by accepting the prize, winner consents to the use of his/her name, age, entry, and/or likeness by sponsors or publicity purposes without further compensation. 4. Prize: A Star Wars galaxy glow-in-the-dark door poster. (Est. retail value of each prize: $4.00). Winners and their legal guardians will be required to sign and return an affidavit of eligibility and liability release. 5. Prize is nontransferable, not returnable, and cannot be sold or redeemed for cash. No substitutions allowed. Taxes on prize are the responsibility of the winner. By accepting the prize, winner agrees that Scholastic Inc. and its respective officers, directors, agents, and employees will have no liability or responsibility for injuries, losses, or damages of any kind resulting from the acceptance, possession, or use of any prize and they will be held harmless against any claims of liability arising directly or indirectly from the prizes awarded. 6. For a list of winners, please send a self-addressed, stamped envelope (residents of RI and VT need not send stamped envelope) to Star Wars Galaxy Poster WINNERS, c/o Scholastic Inc., P. O. Box 7500, Jefferson City, MO 65102 after 9/22/98.

ESSAY QUESTION (100 words or less): What would have happened to Luke Skywalker, Han Solo, Princess Leia Organa, and the Rebellion if Darth Vader had never existed?

☐ BOY ☐ GIRL

Name _____

Address ___ (Please print clearly in ink) _____

City _____ State _____ Zip Code _____

(___) _____

Telephone Number _____ Birthday: Mo./Day/Yr. _____

Mail essay and register receipts verifying the purchase of all three Star Wars Journal titles to:
Star Wars Galaxy Poster Contest, c/o Scholastic Inc., P.O. Box 7500, Jefferson City, MO 65102.

SWC798